For the best dogs in the universe

—A.C. & G.S.

Text copyright © 2017 by Alan Cumming
Jacket art and interior illustrations copyright © 2017 by Grant Shaffer

All rights reserved. Published in the United States by Random House Children's Books, a division of
Penguin Random House LLC, New York.

Random House and the colophon are registered trademarks of Penguin Random House LLC.

Visit us on the Web! randomhousekids.com

Educators and librarians, for a variety of teaching tools, visit us at RHTeachersLibrarians.com

Library of Congress Cataloging-in-Publication Data is available upon request.

ISBN 978-0-399-55797-2 (trade) — ISBN 978-0-399-55798-9 (lib. bdg.) — ISBN 978-0-399-55799-6 (ebook)

MANUFACTURED IN CHINA

10 9 8 7 6 5 4 3 2 1

First Edition

The Adventures of HONEY & LEON

by
Alan Cumming

illustrated by
Grant Shaffer

Random House   New York

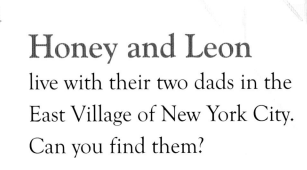

Honey and Leon
live with their two dads in the
East Village of New York City.
Can you find them?

Honey is a rescue mutt, but her days in the pound are *far* behind her. She now has a very posh English accent. Leon, a Chihuahua from Brooklyn, could never quite figure out how Honey came to have such a highfalutin voice, considering she'd been a stray. Honey always explains that she is an actress—and as every actress knows, you gotta have a gimmick!

Honey and Leon have a lovely life, except for one thing . . . their dads go away a lot, traveling for work. An *awful* lot.

Honey and Leon get very sad when their dads leave. Sad because they miss them, of course, but mostly because they aren't able to guard them and keep them out of danger. That's what dogs do! That's what dogs are for! Just ask one.

One baking-hot summer day, Honey and Leon were lying in front of the air conditioner.

Well, actually, she's in front of the AC, but I'm left out in the, er...hot!

Suddenly Honey's ears pricked up.
Before Leon could ask her what she'd
heard, she bounded out of the room!

What is it, Honey? Do you
need bark-up? Oh well,
I'll just stay here and
enjoy the cool.

Honey returned to the living room
to tell Leon the gloomy news.

"Not again!" Leon wailed. "Don't they know we have a job to do?"

"That's it—we have to follow them," said Honey. "It's the only way to keep them safe."

"But we're their dogs," Leon reminded her. "They'll recognize us!"

Honey's eyes lit up. "Not necessarily."

A little while later, Honey and Leon
said a sad goodbye to their dads.

As soon as the apartment door closed, Honey and Leon
rushed to the window to make sure the dads were gone . . .

. . . and quickly packed their bags.

Operation Follow-the-Dads began!
They hurried out and hailed a taxi.

Soon they were on their way.

TAXI
We do live in a gorgeous city, Leon! Parting is such sweet sorrow!
We'll always have New York, Honey. But sometimes a dog's gotta do what a dog's gotta do.

Honey and Leon slipped into two empty seats at the back of the plane.

The flight took the whole night long . . .

. . . and in the morning Honey and Leon got to work.

Following their dads was more
fun than they expected.

Everywhere their dads went,
Honey and Leon followed—always in
disguise and alert to any danger.

When the dads went for a sail on a yacht,
Honey and Leon followed in a dinghy.

But the biggest challenge of all came that night. Honey and Leon were going to a VERY fancy party!

Threats were everywhere!
People! Cars! Flashing
lights! Loud noises!

Suddenly Honey heard photographers
shouting at a lady on the red carpet . . .

LOOK THIS WAY, HONEY!

OVER HERE, HONEY!

ONE MORE, HONEY!

. . . and though she knew she was meant to be
guarding the dads, she just couldn't resist.

Leon couldn't believe his eyes!
What was she thinking?

The next day, Honey was the talk of the town!

The dogs spent the rest of the day trying to keep
Honey's star status hidden from the dads.

Finally the trip came to an end, and Honey and Leon
snuck back to the airport.

Honey and Leon made it home
in the nick of time. And to think
their dads would never know!
But just like all families,
this one has its secrets.